RICK AND ROCKY

By **Paula S. Rowan**

Illustrated by **Catherine Myler Fruisen**

ISBN 0-7683-2175-1

Text copyright © Paula S. Rowan
Illustrations by Catherine Myler Fruisen
Art copyright © 1999 Design Press Books
All rights reserved.

Published in 2000 by Cedco Publishing Company
100 Pelican Way, San Rafael, California 94901
For a free catalog of other Cedco® products, please write to the address
above, or visit our website: www.cedco.com

Book and jacket design by Janice Shay

This is a Design Press book.
Design Press is a division of the Savannah College of Art and Design.

Printed in China

1 3 5 7 9 10 8 6 4 2

*For all the artists I have known at the
Savannah College of Art and Design*

PAULA S. ROWAN

───────────────

For Rick and Rocky

CATHERINE MYLER FRUISEN

Rocky the cat is Rick's
best friend.
They live in a house just
'round the bend.
Rocky is black and white (and green),
The fattest cat you've ever seen!
Rick is a boy with eyes of blue.
He's happy and smart (a lot like you).

This young boy
   and his feline friend
Play all day,
   from beginning to end.

Rock loves to chase a white paper ball
Tossed by Rick to the end of the hall.

With a slip

and a slide,

a jump and a fall,

Rock dives at Rick's feet,

then runs up the wall!

After the game of chase is through,
   They have a tasty chore to do.

It's time to feed Rick's golden fish.
YUM! thinks Rocky, That looks DEE-lish!

Fat as he is, he's feeling thinner

And meows to Rick, "It's time for dinner!"

They both enjoy their favorite feast—

Puff pops and milk,

for a boy and his beast.

Rick's evening bath comes right before bed.
Far from a chore, it's fun instead!
Rick towels dry from bottom to top,
As Rocky licks each drippy drop.

This good cat deserves a treat
For drying off a little boy's feet.
Rock's bedtime snack is nicer than mice—
It's a bowl full of slippery cubes of ice!

Now our Rick lays down his head.
But guess who else is in his bed?
Comfy and cozy, the pals snooze away....
'Til Rocky begins to dream of play,
Running and pouncing, try after try—
Batting his paws at a whizzing pop fly!

Wide-awake Rocky thinks now would be fine
For a game of catch—in spite of the time!
Gently he pats Rick right on the nose,
Waking the boy from his peaceful doze.

"Oh, my gosh, it's half past two!
Be still!" Rick yells, "I'm warning you!"
But scolding means zip to this naughty cat
Who has lately become a major brat.

Neither book nor pillow can make him stop.

He roars, **"MEOW"** 'til Rick's ears pop!

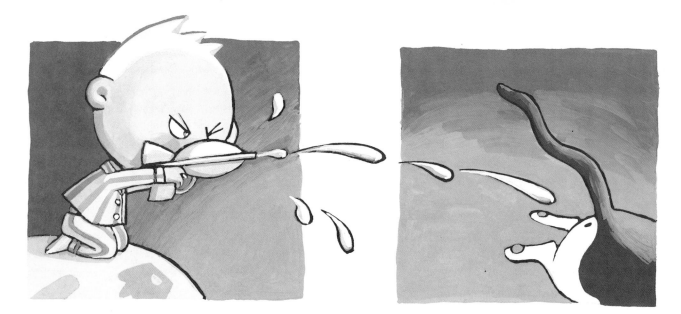

"That's it," says Rick. "It's all-out war!"
Picking his squirt gun up from the floor.

But Rock takes revenge, and it's astronomic,
Ripping to shreds Rick's favorite comic.

To that, Rick responds with his weapon of choice:
The vacuum cleaner's FEROCIOUS voice!

Rock hides in the chest behind Rick's clothes,
Away from the troll with the noisy nose.

Though tempted with treats,
   Rock won't come out—
He'd rather twitch his tail and pout.
Rick even offers his small golden fish,
But all he can hear is Rock's tail go SWISH.

Rick glumly kicks the white paper ball,
He's lonely and sad and can't sleep at all.
But, wait! There's a squeak—who could it be?
His pal is back, THE GREAT ROCKY!

There *IS* no game that cat loves more
Than chasing balls across the floor.

They play until their eyelids droop,
Then leap in bed with one last whoop.
This time, they both fall fast asleep—
Off to dreamland without a peep.

In dreams, where ANYthing can be,
Rick sees himself as royalty.
The King of Baseball waves his bat
To the purring Prince,
his favorite cat.

Rock dreams of soaring high in flight—
A cat and his boy, what a magical sight!
He and Rick make a perfect match
    For a flying game
        of moonlight catch.

Will he wake Rick up again to play?
We'll save that tale for another day....

Rocky the cat is Rick's best friend.

Together, their stories will never end!